Mullins Collection of Best New Horror

EDITED BY

Aaron Mullins

This is a work of fiction. Names, characters, organisations, places, events and incidents are either products of the author's imagination or are used fictitiously. Any resemblance to actual persons, living or dead, or actual events is purely coincidental.

ISBN: 9781730883675

PRAISE FOR AARON MULLINS

"Tales of mythical beasties tops charts"
Troon Times

"The book was **a top 10 bestseller**... sitting alongside books by
Neil Gaiman and Stephen King"
The Orkney News

"These short stories just pull you in from the very first page.
Brilliant stories with something for everyone to enjoy"
Amazon Review

"It has already featured in the Amazon top 100 bestsellers...
alongside books by Stephen King and Dean Koontz"
Press and Journal

"If you love **suspense with good humour** then look no further"
Amazon Review

"**Very well written**, as you would expect from an Aaron Mullins book, and
gives you just enough of a tingle down your spine!!"
Amazon Review

"...engrossing and **entertaining collection** of short stories ...would make a
five-star-rating popular TV drama series
...universal storytelling at its best"
– Review by Carol McKay (author and reader for The Highland Book Prize) of
Mysteries and Misadventures: Tales from the Highlands

"His love for the Highlands and its people shines through, both in his
stories and reflections on his personal journey"
Caithness Courier

"They arrive like sprites. Whispering in his ear, buzzing around in his
mind, walking around his consciousness, forcing their way into his
thoughts. The shadows at the edge, the inspiration for his next writing
project"
Ayrshire Magazine (Interview with Aaron Mullins)

AARON MULLINS

DEDICATION

This book is for those who embrace the night.
Even Batman does his best work in the dark.

AARON MULLINS

AARON MULLINS

FICTION

Mysteries and Misadventures: Tales from the Highlands
Scottish Urban Legends: 50 Myths and True Stories
Scottish Legends: 55 Mythical Monsters
Scottish Killers: 25 True Crime Stories
Mullins Collection of Best New Fiction
Mullins Collection of Best New Horror

WRITING GUIDES

How to Write Fiction: A Creative Writing Guide for Authors

BUSINESS GUIDES

How to Write a Business Plan
The Ultimate Business Plan Template

PSYCHOLOGY

The Effect of Mate Value on Self-esteem
Social Responsibility and Community Resilience
Risk Perception in Extreme Event Decision Making
Ethnic Differences in Perceptions of Social Responsibility
and many more…

www.aaronmullins.com

AARON MULLINS

PREFACE

Four short horror stories with a twist. Stay up late with the twisted minds of four authors whose aim is to tell short horror stories that send a chill down the spine of their readers. Tales that have you checking underneath the bed... or wondering whether that shadow in the corner just moved.

In this collection you will find short stories from the early writing careers of four horror authors, all guaranteed to instil a feeling of dread deep into your bones as your shaking fingers struggle to turn the page.

A dark secret is revealed in *My Natalie*, a tale of vengeful love. A home with a hidden past threatens to destroy a young family in *The House*. The restless spirit of a young girl has to deliver an important message in *Phantom Memory*. Finally, thrill-seeking Melanie gets more than she bargained for as she explores the mysterious festival in *The Secrets of Hidden Places*.

A short, thrilling journey through four horror stories that reflect the stage each author had reached with their craft, captured in time as they emerge into the world of writing.

We hope you enjoy taking this terrifying journey with us.
And the horrors that await you.

Aaron Mullins

www.aaronmullins.com

CONTENTS

1. MY NATALIE

Angela Kelman

'My darling Natalie, you've always kept me warm. I've not felt the same heat since you left, until now. This feeling, right now, it's addictive. I'm addicted to you; there is no other way to describe my love. But you put the fire out you see, when you left, left me cold, alone – how could you... It never used to be a one-sided affair.'

'But you're just like the others, it seems. You play with my mind.'

'I didn't think I would ever invite you down here, not *you*.'

'Our time together was happy, wasn't it? I'd mapped out our paths to ambitions from the same inspirations we shared. Couples in love do that, don't they? They share everything. It was all shattered when you walked away from us. You didn't even look back that day.'

'I forgive you for that now.'

'Do I love you too much? Perhaps? Though it doesn't matter anymore. I can cherish you forever now - and I will, don't worry. Now you have come back to me.'

'Oh, Natalie, I've never forgotten how you smelt – so sweet. I've been thinking about it a lot lately.'

'And it is *my* smell, not his.'

'It's fading now, I hate that! Even now as I clutch you close to me. Always fading. Like petals, falling from a rose.'

'Sorry, do you mind if I touch you?'

'The feel of your skin under my fingers is just as smooth as it was, as I

1

remember it to be. Oh, how I will miss the shape of your curves. But I will not forget them, just like I will never forget your voice. When I close my eyes I can hear it. I can hear you say my name over and over. And I can watch you. I can see you move to me, every day.'

'That will never fade.'

'Ahh listen, listen do you hear? It's our song. You loved the record player, remember. The old fashioned crackle, that's what you liked. It reminds me of when we first met. I still picture your face you know, your full lips smiling at me through the cigarette smoke. Your hair fell perfectly over your shoulders. It still holds its copper tone, even now – it's beautiful. And it will move again with me, when I move, when we dance together again.'

'We laughed so much that night.'

'What is it, dear? Don't look at me like that, please. It was just too late for you to apologise. I can't listen to apologies that aren't meant, and I knew your love was gone. Gone to him. Him. What did he do to you? Turned you against me.'

'You know it pains me to keep you here in the shadows of my life. I'd rather you were with me, to carry you on my arm with pride again. Still, only floorboards separate us, dear. We are together really - how it should be. And happy memories – we will have more. You will look nice here, nicer than the others.'

'I will close your eyes now.'

'And I will be careful with you. I promise. And you will keep me warm again, my darling love. My Natalie.'

2. THE HOUSE

Gary Steward

It was cold, so cold.

When the agent showed us around that dark February evening it hadn't registered. Then again, it was minus three outside. I remember the frost billowing from Jan's mouth, her cheeks red from the biting cold wind. Most of all I remember the excitement that shone from her face; it illuminated the dark hallway. I'd tried to remain calm and logical, nodding my head to the sales patter whilst inside I was bursting. I could not suppress the giggle of delight when we saw what would be the nursery. Jan had spun in the middle of the dusty room with her fingers on our 'bump'.

It was perfect.

Now I wish I'd never laid eyes on the house. Looking back I remember thinking the agent seemed to be in a hurry to get out of the place; her fingers fumbled as she tried to lock the door and her heels slithered on the ice rutted driveway as she scurried to her car.

*

It took three months for the deal to go through; our buyers were the most awkward people imaginable as they dragged their heels over every little detail. Then, one morning in May, it was ours. The contrast to that first viewing couldn't have been greater. The leaves on the beech trees were that bright green colour that only lasts for a few weeks, before they begin their final dance with the sun and fade to autumn brown. I insisted that Jan sit and do nothing other than make endless cups of tea for the removal men, but of course she couldn't resist and soon had the vacuum cleaner reaching into dusty carpeted corners. Windows were thrown open and fresh air billowed in carrying scents of freshly mown grass from a neighbour's lawn. Sunlight sparkled on the stream that bordered on the edge of the garden.

It wasn't until the men left that I noticed it again, the cold. The boiler was temperamental, we knew that, but even after it sputtered into life it couldn't shift the icy spots that lurked, especially upstairs. I didn't know a great deal about the history of the house other than the previous owner was an elderly widow. We assumed she had been frugal with the heating and it would take time to warm the place again.

I know now that houses have feelings too.

*

It was the third morning that it began. I was downstairs in the kitchen making tea and toast when I heard Jan scream. The sound of her tumbling, the rumble of her body on the stairs will haunt me forever. I found her in a heap in the hallway; her legs twisted on the bottom two steps. Jan was dazed and whimpering, her hands cradling our bump. She lay there for several minutes until she felt able to rise. I helped her stand. We made it to the lounge where she lay on the couch. I came back after calling the doctor and saw the puzzlement on her face. She told me she'd been pushed. Then she clutched her stomach as the pain began.

Josh arrived that evening. He was early but well despite his trauma. I forgot everything and held them both so tight.

It was going to be fine.

*

The days warmed up, the house seemed welcoming as friends and relatives visited in a constant stream of well wishing. I remember noticing a thoughtful look in Jan's eyes occasionally and she was always extra careful on the stairs. We didn't discuss what happened that day, until later.

*

It was late June when our best friends, Paul and Catherine, came to stay

4

for a week with their two year old daughter, Bella. Josh still slept in our room and Bella had a cot with her parents in what would be the nursery down the long corridor. I'd spent hours painting that room, making it bright and welcoming. Clouds covered the walls and ceiling, with a cheeky-faced sun peeking through. Yet no matter how bright the sunshine outside, the room remained dingy. We thought it must be the tree outside whose branches sometimes scratched the window when the wind blew.

That first evening with our friends was wonderful. The babies were fast asleep and two baby monitors sat on chair arms. We chatted and listened to music while birdsong drifted in through the open patio doors. I'd just opened a second bottle of wine when we heard it. The sound of breathing coming from our friends' baby monitor.

But this wasn't the breath of a sleeping baby.

It was deeper, harsher and carried the hint of threat.

I ran upstairs with Paul and we opened the bedroom door. All was peaceful. Bella was fast asleep, but her head was twisted slightly and had somehow slipped beneath her pillow. She woke slowly and sleepily asked for a drink of water.

The relief we felt banished any fears. Paul suggested it must have been the breeze outside that we'd heard. I agreed but didn't mention that the leaves on the tree were perfectly still. One other odd thing was a smell in the room, a mature smell, musty and unpleasant. We put it down to the age of the house and let Bella sleep once more, though back downstairs the conversation was muted as ears listened for any noise. Not long after, everyone decided to call it a night.

The next morning I was awake early. I made breakfast and Jan joined me in her robe with Josh in her arms. She sat and opened her gown to feed him, and his contented gurgles were a joy. Our friends were late rising but eventually we heard sounds from above and the flush of the loo. They came in for breakfast and were oddly quiet as they helped Bella with her breakfast, sharing the occasional glance with each other. At last Paul cleared his throat and spoke. He asked us, quite seriously, if there was anyone else straying in the house with us. I said of course not – who else could there be?

Paul and Catherine looked at one another again, and then Paul spoke. Last night, he described, after we were all in bed, he woke feeling very cold. It was dark in the room but he could see a shadow by the cot, a figure. The outline suggested an old woman bent over Bella, looking at her intently. He had pulled the duvet back and the movement made whatever it was vanish.

All that remained was a musty smell. He lifted Bella and placed her in bed with his wife who hadn't woken at all.

They were clearly spooked by this and said that they wouldn't be staying any longer if we didn't mind. They'd decided to drive over to see his parents instead.

The remainder of breakfast was a strained affair and they left soon after, having already packed their bags before breakfast. We did meet up with them again, but never at our house.

*

A month or so later, we bought a dog, a rescue animal from a local shelter. It was of indeterminate breed and age, but very placid and gentle. He was called Alfie and he doted on the baby, spending hours by the cot fast asleep. Those first months flew by and the house became warmer. After the unease caused by our friends' concern we gradually became used to the house's eccentricities. Doors would open or close without reason, things would appear in unexpected places and we jokingly put it down to 'Mrs Wotsit'. No harm came to anyone.

At least, not then.

*

Our first Christmas arrived and with it the first real snowfall for years. Josh was now beginning to crawl and sit up without falling over and he laughed constantly, when he wasn't crying of course. I remember reading to him, or maybe just talking as he lay in his cot with eyes transfixed on the mobile which hung above his head. Once he had closed his eyes I quietly left the room.

I swear I checked the catches on the side of the cot.

Later, when Jan and I were in the lounge writing a pile of Christmas cards with a glass of wine, the dog began to growl. I told him to shush, but the hackles on his back were rigid. I'd never seen him do this before and his eyes were fixed on the slightly open lounge door. I stood to investigate and it was then we heard Josh cry, but not on the baby monitor. I rushed into the hall and there he was sat at the top of the stairs looking confused. As I moved towards him he suddenly toppled forwards and I only just managed to catch him, before he tumbled all the way down.

The dog was beside himself and ran upstairs to the nursery where he barked for some time as Josh cried in Jan's arms. I ran my hands over the catches on the cot and both were undone. I looked at Jan and told her that I was certain they were secure when I left Josh. The locks were quite stiff and there was no way he could have opened them himself, even by accident. It took some time to quieten everyone down, but Josh slept with us after that.

*

It was the spring of the following year when it happened. I'd gone into work early and was driving home in the afternoon when my mobile rang. Jan's voice was hysterical; she couldn't find Josh. My driving bordered on reckless as I negotiated the traffic and left the car door swinging open as I dashed into the house. I could hear Jan's frantic voice calling out his name again and again to the sound of doors opening. I ran upstairs to meet her and she fell into my arms, her face strained beyond recognition and wet with tears. I tried to calm her and in between sobs she told me she'd left Josh alone for only two minutes to prepare a snack. He'd been sitting on the lounge floor surrounded by coloured building bricks. When she came back, he'd gone.

We began to search together, desperately looking in even the most ridiculous of places. He'd begun to walk recently and his boundaries had extended, but not by much. I was on the verge of calling the police when I noticed Alfie sitting by the back door which opened onto the garden. I don't know why I hadn't seen him before. His eyes were fixed on the handle and he barked as I approached. I wrenched the door open and he bounded onto the sloping lawn that led down to the stream. Jan was close behind me calling out his name. My mind was in turmoil as the sound of the fast flowing water grew louder; there'd been heavy rains recently. I'd intended to make the rickety fence secure this summer when Josh would be out here more. I prayed I hadn't been too late.

Alfie found him first. Josh was sitting on the river bank pulling up handfuls of grass and trying to eat it. He looked happy and smiled as Jan picked him up in her arms. She sank to the ground and rocked him back and forth as she sobbed out his name while Alfie capered about barking. It was then that I noticed the musty smell, even out here in the fresh air. Two of Josh's building bricks floated down the stream, bobbing along with the strong current.

That day I decided to delve deeper into the history of our house. The nearest neighbours had always kept to themselves, hidden behind trees and shrubs and we'd been too busy to cultivate friendships. When I questioned them they'd been vague, but eventually one did mention that the old lady who'd lived there had been childless and had taken an unusual interest in their own young children when they were little. They gave me the address of a distant relative of hers and after some searching I found a telephone number. The elderly lady I contacted was helpful and welcomed the opportunity to chat. She told me that her relative had been childless, but not through choice. Several miscarriages had made her bitter to the point of jealousy and after the death of her husband she had become more reclusive. I thanked her and put down the phone, a chill gripping my insides.

*

I put the house on the market within the week. It sold quickly, which wasn't surprising as it was an attractive property, at least on the outside. I hadn't the slightest qualm of misgiving when the keys were handed over, no sense of guilt or remorse, but then the new owners were an older couple with no children.

We moved to another part of town and eventually my work took me across the country. Josh had a sister by now, and that dreadful period was a distant memory that we never discussed again.

*

I did have reason to go back once more earlier this year. An old client needed advice so I made it into an overnight stop. The following morning I turned the car to head north and home, but on impulse took a detour. As I pulled onto the familiar street it was transformed. The house was gone and in its place the beginnings of a new building. Men in hard yellow hats drove diggers over the rutted earth; rows of timber lay by the stream alongside pallets of bricks and large sacks of cement. I stopped and asked one of the builders what it was going to be. I explained that I used to live in the old house. His reply made my blood run cold.

It was going to be a nursery.

3. PHANTOM MEMORY

Aaron Mullins

She's here again. I can see her in the mirror, her pale skin and torn dress reflecting the meagre light from the bedside candle. Her young hand clutching the arm of the smiling brown bear that I gave her for her eighth birthday the year before. The bear has lost an eye. White stuffing tumbles from the ripped stitching across its neck, turning its once comforting face into a sagging, manic grin.

The razor falls from my hand and clatters noisily in the sink. *She knows I can see her.* She knows too that I can see the shape of the dresser behind her, visible through her near transparent form. With a trembling hand I turn off the tap and our eyes hold each other's gaze in the silence. I know what she's about to do, but I'm not ready for it.

A pain builds in my head, forcing out the breath I'd been holding in a choked gasp. I quickly gulped another lungful.

Go away.

I hold the thought and close my eyes as I did yesterday, and the day before.

One...

My chest tightens. *What if it doesn't work this time?* A jolt of panic shakes through my body, rushing blood deafening inside my head.

Two...

An ache gnaws the pit of my stomach, threatening to empty its contents onto the tiled floor. It's the third day she's come. Rosie. My daughter. *Or what's left of her.* A phantom girl who will never see her ninth birthday.

With her comes the weakness. I haven't the energy to leave the house, a blanket of fatigue heavy upon me, confining me to my bed. But rest doesn't come easy. She makes me have dreams. *Or more precisely, one dream.* A snippet of memory played on a loop every time I sleep.

Her memory.

She's walking along a street, her small hand held gently by another, a man clouded in shadow. *So happy.* They turn to take a shortcut through an alleyway, the darkness swallowing them both. They're almost at the end when he appears, his stance menacing, the blade in his hand glinting as it catches the light from the moon.

The clouded man takes a step to protect the girl but he's struck and stumbles, slumping against the wall, the knife penetrating his chest. The terrified scream of a child pierces the night.

The screaming is cut short as the attacker grabs her, clamping one hand firmly over her mouth and nose as he squeezes her neck with the other. She kicks out, catching his shin, forcing him to relinquish the grip on her throat.

But the relief is short-lived as he snatches her ponytail and smashes her face into the wall, her young nose cracking with the force of the blow. Blood pours over her lips, trickles down her chin and splashes onto her dress.

He's behind her now, his weight crushing her fragile body against the wall. He draws his knife and kneels down beside her body. Then darkness.

Three...

I open my eyes.

She's gone.

*

I wake with a jolt, a scream still echoing from my throat, sheets damp with sweat. I look around, finally recognising I'm still at home, still in my cottage in the countryside. Still alone.

I catch my breath and rise from the bed. I walk to the sink in the bathroom, averting my eyes from the mirror as I turn the tap. The cool water is refreshing as I cup it in my hands and splash it on my face, washing away her lingering memory.

I feel cold.

Not again, she's never appeared twice in one night before.

I hear the click of the door closing behind me. My back stiffens, my arms suspended in the air clutching the towel. The creeping chill pinches my face.

I'm not alone.

I slowly lift my gaze to the mirror and look behind me. She's there. In the reflection a pale hand reaches out to touch my arm. I throw myself against the wall, sending shockwaves down my spine.

"What do you want? Rosie... you... you're dead," I scream at the seemingly empty room, the high-pitched edge of terror gripping my voice.

A footstep is taken towards me.

I shrink back, hugging the wall. A sigh echoes around the room, misting the glass on the mirror. Then a watery squeak. A word appears across the mirror, written by an unseen hand.

Follow.

"F-follow you w-where?" I shriek, my nerves failing, eyes darting around the room. The door swings open with a crash, signalling my answer. I fall to the floor and tears soon follow, body shaking.

Another crash, the bedroom door near breaking its hinges. *She's angrier than before.* Realising I've no choice but to follow, I rise unsteadily to my feet. A wave of nausea washes over me; vomit catches in my throat, ready to spew forth from my dry mouth. I swallow it.

Crash! The door to the outside world is flung wide, sending a cold breeze howling through the cottage. With it comes a surge of emotion that steals my breath. I take a step forwards and find my body now holds a new vigour, the lethargy of the past few days seeming to have passed. With my newfound strength I pull on my coat, grab the small torch from the drawer and walk out into the night.

I peer into the gloom. She's waiting by the gate, her body glowing faintly in the light of the waning moon. I walk towards her. She begins to run up the hill, away from the cottage.

"Rosie, wait, I can't..." I call out to her and quicken my pace, the hood of my coat flapping fiercely in the wind which snatches away the rest of my words. She stops and looks back over her shoulder. She then slowly raises her arm and extends a finger in the direction of a nearby hill. Then she's gone.

I stumble along the stony path until I reach the place she disappeared and turn my gaze to the direction she'd pointed. Fear seeps into my bones as my eyes settle on where I must go. The small cemetery on the outskirts of the village. The seclusion that had been a blessing when we first moved here now feels like a dreadful isolation.

I make my way up the winding path past the tall, gnarled trees that line the route to the village cemetery. Eventually I reach the large, rusted iron gates that signal the entrance to the resting place of the dead. I pause a moment to catch my breath before pushing one of the gates. After initial resistance it opens with an ominous creak, telling all who may be listening of my arrival. I step cautiously through the gate, eyes scanning all around as I move.

I look across the sea of headstones. In the dim light I make out movement near one of the graves a few rows up. I head towards it. As I draw near it becomes apparent what the movement is, a white rose hovering in the air, gently spinning above the grave. As I approach it falls to the ground.

Suddenly she appears, solemnly staring at me from behind the gravestone. I crouch down and switch on the torch, pulling my coat tight to shelter from the wind as I read the inscription.

Here lies Rosie Baker. Died 12th November 2011 aged 8. May she find peace with her father in heaven.

My body goes deathly still.

"With her father in heaven? But... I'm not..." I look up at her for answers. A voice drifts into my head. A solitary word.

Remember.

"Remember what? I don't understand," I shout, trying to carry my voice above the rising wind. She walks to the next headstone, pauses, and then motions for me to follow. She points to it and begins to silently cry.

I crouch in front of it, focus the torch and read the inscription. I jump back, my mind screaming the words I'd just read.

Here lies Edward Baker. Died 12th November 2011 aged 39. May he find peace with his daughter in heaven.

I drop the torch and fall onto the earth covering the grave. *My grave.*

Suddenly the memory is upon me. Her memory. *Our memory.* We're walking along the street. I'm gently holding her hand. *We're happy.* We turn to take a shortcut through a darkened alleyway. We're approaching the end when a man steps into our path. I see the blade and move quickly to protect her, but I'm too slow and the knife pierces my heart. I fall dead against the wall.

"How could I have forgotten? I'm sorry, Rosie, I'm so, so sorry," I cry into the night. *But why am I still here?* Rosie's voice drifts into my mind. *You would not let go of life, father. They sent me back for you. Follow me now.*

"I will, I will. Show me," I beg. A small hand grips my own. All fear is gone. *It's her. My daughter Rosie.* She smiles at me, the sweet happy smile of an eight year old girl finally reunited with her father. I smile back. Suddenly we're lifting and floating upwards, heading into a light that burns bright, but does not pain the eyes. It radiates love. I put my arms around her and hold her tight as we ascend.

"You're safe now. I promise," I whisper into her ear, and with that we are gone.

4. THE SECRETS OF HIDDEN PLACES

Kate Robinson

The Festival was held in the dying days of summer.

The personality of the Island changed during the Festival, opening the gates for all things to pass. All women were beautiful and all men were prosperous. It was a time of magic. Men found long lost brothers, great treasures and made dangerous promises. Not all who saw it start would see it end.

Melanie took a deep breath through her mouth to avoid smelling the rank stench of the water and almost choked when she tasted it instead. The boat tipped on the grey water, leaning as if to capsize before rolling back. Hanging over the railing, Melanie spat out the bile that rose up. When she was certain that the sour taste and the burn in her throat were all that remained, she leaned back. The wind blew multi-coloured hair into her eyes and raised goosebumps down her back. She pulled her artistically ripped leather jacket tighter. It was big enough to fit around her and then some; it had belonged to her father before he had died and was nearly as old as she was. She pulled it up and buried her nose in its sweet smell of leather, perfume and an almost familiar scent that Melanie was positive was her dad. Her pocket buzzed and she reached in, feeling around the sweet wrappers and coins for her phone, already knowing who the message was from.

'You better be on the boat. I've promised Felix that you'd go with her on the coaster. We'll meet you at the docks luv Laura :)'

Melanie flicked back through her texts from Laura. A week of texts about how wonderful the Festival was, about how much fun she would have if she came. They had finally convinced her to join them for the weekend.

'I hear it's haunted.'

Melanie glanced up at the boy who had spoken. He was entertaining his group of friends. 'It's got the record for the most accidents, it must be haunted.'

He was talking about the permanent fairground on the Island's waterfront. Melanie always found it odd that holding a world record for fatal accidents could attract people to the island, as well as repel them. Melanie sighed to herself, she was positive she could come up with excuses to avoid the coaster once she was at the fairground.

The Island was close now; she could hear the music coming from the fairground. The noise from the crowded boat became louder; kids became restless while mothers shouted and fathers scolded. Melanie reached into her pocket and pulled out her headphones. Slipping them into her ears, she turned up the volume and tried to lose herself in the music. The boat bumped against the dock and Melanie squeaked, lost her footing and tumbled against the back of a man. He turned and looked at her with irritation. She lowered her eyes and rubbed her hands on her skirt.

Stepping onto still ground, Melanie scanned the crowd for familiar faces. Even on the Island during the magic time of the Festival, when the strange and unique were commonplace, her friends would still stand out.

They weren't here.

She considered waiting but the magic of the Island tugged at her; she decided to find something to eat before searching further. She wandered along the promenade, where stalls and shops lined the way, their wares spilling out onto the pavement and their music spiraling up to the sky. She walked past stalls selling hotdogs and burgers, continued past one selling donuts. She craved something richer, something special. She decided to explore the wider area and turned off the promenade down a narrow alley. The stink of salt water wasn't quite so strong down here, something else permeated the air – the rich and unmistakable smell of roasting meat.

The stall was so small she could easily have missed it. Painted a red so dark it was almost black. Lighter red paint spelt out the name *Neifelhiem*.

The small girl minding the stall was narrow and pale, her short dark hair teased into an artful mess. She watched Melanie the way a fox watches a rabbit.

'Hi,' Melanie said. The girl looked at her, but didn't make any effort to smile or speak. Melanie didn't notice, she was too busy reading the notices behind the girl. The writing was faded, the letters swirled in strange ways, the words an illegible jumble. A myriad of bottles lined the shelves under the notices. Shoes ran along the bottom of the stall. A collection of headphones and personal music players hung from a hook in the wall. Mobile phones were stacked on a shelf. One small wall was littered with overlapping posters; faces of missing people staring out with dead eyes.

'Do you want something?' The girl in the stall finally spoke. 'Food perhaps?' Melanie nodded. The girl turned and opened an ancient oven. The smell of roasting meat poured out, wrapping itself around the stall, shielding it from the reek of seawater.

'You sell weird stuff,' Melanie said, relaxing into one of the tall seats arranged haphazardly in front of the stall.

'We sell a lot of second-hand goods.' The girl looked up from her oven and stared hard at Melanie. 'My name is Nit. I run the stall for Balor.'

The girl stood up and offered a thin pale hand.

'I'm Melanie,' Melanie said, taking the girl's hand. Self-control stopped her from flinching at Nit's hand clammy and bone-cold hand. As she pulled back Melanie could not resist the urge to wipe her hand on her skirt. 'Where do you get all this stuff?' Nit smiled again and for a second Melanie had the impression of teeth that were too long to fit inside a human mouth. But the notion vanished as quickly as it had occurred and Nit was just a girl again.

'Are you interested in buying something?' Nit asked crouching in front of the oven.

Melanie laughed. 'The boots look good.' She pointed to a pair of neon pink doc martins. 'But I'm not here to buy shoes.' Nit passed her a shank of meat in a small Styrofoam tray. Melanie sniffed at it; it was lamb with the juices still bubbling. Her stomach growled. The meat burnt her fingers but she didn't care. She tore into it with her teeth, almost groaning as it fell softly from the bone.

'Do you want a drink with that?' Nit asked. Melanie nodded and swallowed.

'Are any of those alcoholic?' Melanie wiped her chin and pointed to the bottles lining the shelves at the back of the stall. Nit nodded. Melanie scrutinised the bottles. The labels were dusty, the corners turning in, most of them torn in places. What writing she could see was pale and faded.

'Any recommendations?' She pulled some more meat off the bone with her fingers and wolfed it down. Licking juices from her fingertips, she smiled and made a mental note to remember this place.

'Actually, yes,' Nit said softly. She peered at Melanie from under dark hair for a long moment. 'I think I know one that would suit you Melanie.' Nit looked away and pulled down a slender green bottle filled with dark liquid. She tipped it up and handed the glass to Melanie.

'What is this?' Melanie looked at the glass in front of her. 'It's purple,' she added. She lifted the glass and sniffed it; it smelt like cloves.

'Monster Blood,' Nit said. Melanie knocked the shot back with a practiced motion. It burned her throat going down, starting a comfortable fire in her belly. She coughed and smacked her lips once. The after taste came upon her slowly and built, smooth and herb ridden. 'What about that one?' She gestured to a bottle that was clear glass and squat, the liquid inside golden with small bubbles.

'Ghouls Treasure.' Nit smiled.

'Can I try it?' Melanie smiled at Nit when she nodded. The heat in her belly swelled and a weakness ran down her arms. Her head swam. Melanie smiled wider and clenched her hands twice to feel the tingle in her fingertips. She sniffed at the new glass handed to her and smelt honey.

'It's mead?' She breathed and sipped it. Like Monster Blood, it went down smoothly with an initial sweetness. The heat grew quicker this time overwhelming the sweetness of the drink. It burned in her stomach and up into her throat. The roasting burn faded quickly however, leaving in its place a soothing warmth and feeling of contentment.

'Do you like it?' Nit asked. Melanie nodded.

'I've always liked things that are a bit different,' she admitted. 'It's gotten me into trouble once or twice.' She picked up the shank and peeled off the last strips of meat with ravenous efficiency; she hadn't realized just how hungry she was.

'I can tell.' Nit smiled, fox-like again. 'I think I should invite you to Alfheim.' Nit's head jerked towards a sign. Melanie squinted at it. The notices which had been indecipherable only a moment ago now looked clearer. The heat in her belly grew and spread down her legs to her toes. The letters faded, going out of focus before coming harshly into focus, dark and clear.

'Alfheim?'

'You can see the sign?'

Melanie nodded.

'It's a bar,' Nit said quietly. 'Below our feet.' Melanie blinked.

'Underground? A cellar bar?' Melanie leaned forwards. 'How do I get in?'

'Balor must see you and grant you permission. Only a select few are permitted,' Nit said 'Are you sure you wish to enter?' Melanie nodded. Nit grinned and disappeared, ducking down beneath the countertop.

'Hey,' Melanie called leaning forward to try and see where Nit had disappeared to. 'Where'd you go?' But Nit was gone; all that was left was old shoes, and dusty bottles. Melanie sat back with a huff. 'Typical.' She looked at her empty glass and bare bone. 'Should have got another.'

Melanie waited and glanced around the eclectic stall, looking for a distraction. Her eyes fell onto the pictures of the missing people. Melanie stared and frowned; the posters overlapped each other so much that they sat an inch thick in places. Some of them were recent, from last year or the year before; others were much older, going back ten or fifteen years. All claimed that the person pictured was last seen at the Festival.

'Must be artistic,' Melanie muttered. 'Morbid though.'

She was contemplating reaching across and refilling her own glass when the stall shook roughly, the wood creaked and a string of curses came up from the thin wood by her feet, followed by a man who stood at almost seven feet tall. He was solidly built with wide shoulders. Melanie did a double take; she could have sat comfortably on just one of this man's shoulders. Like with Nit and the image of the fox, she had a sudden flash of tarnished metal armor on this man. The giant man turned and glared at her with one terrifying eye, the other covered by yellowing cloth. His face was a mass of creases and half-hidden by a scraggly beard. He was dressed in stained white clothing, and further food stains covered the apron he was wiping his hands on. He grunted and leaned forward.

'Melanie.' His voice was that of a giant, deep and loud. Melanie was glad to see Nit clambering up from the basement alongside him.

'Yes.' Nit dipped her head not looking at his face. The huge man stared at Melanie for a long moment before grunting and moving with surprising speed back beneath the counter.

'How did he do that?' Melanie asked when she was sure he had gone. Nit smiled, but her hands were shaking.

'Balor does many things, including fitting into spaces he should not.' She stepped over and opened a small door at the side of the stall.

'Come, but be careful, the way is treacherous,' warned Nit.

Melanie hopped down from her stool and followed Nit. The floor inside was littered with the old shoes as she had seen from the counter.

'Go down,' Nit gave her a small push.

'Um how?' she asked.

'You must remove your shoes,' Nit said. Melanie frowned. 'Or you will not be allowed to enter. Balor is very strict about shoes.'

Melanie sighed and considered backing out, but she unlaced her boots. They were old and worn and her big toe was starting to press out of her right boot. In a few months it would have broken through and she would have to get new ones, or rather new second-hand ones. She slipped off her boots and hoped Nit didn't notice the fact that her fishnet tights had ripped on her big toes. Her tights did not protect her against the cold and she shivered when her feet touched the stone.

'Also any phones, mp3 players, any other technology items you've got.'

'Do I sign for them?' Melanie asked as Nit gave her a small burlap bag.

'If you want, but I'll remember which ones are yours – I always remember what belonged to whom,' Nit shrugged, taking the bag back from Melanie's trembling fingers. 'Be careful.' Nit leaned forwards under the counter and slid a barely visible door back. It was just about large enough for Melanie to fit through and again she wondered how Balor had managed it.

Melanie squatted down and shuffled forwards. She banged her head on the wood of the counter before ducking through the door. Once through, it opened up into a steep tunnel. The floor was slippery inside. The air was damp and stank of mildew. She lost her footing almost instantly. The walls were bare brick and rough on her groping hands. She managed to get purchase but ended up with her legs sliding out in front of her. She gave up and went onto her bum with a small bump. She struggled to get to her feet like Bambi on the ice. Nit closed the small door behind her.

'Come on Alice,' Melanie mumbled still clinging to the wall. 'The rabbit hole awaits.' She forced herself to stand and in a stumbling slide she made her way down the tunnel. The slope was severe enough that she could have easily slid down on her bum like a small child at the park. But her skirt was short and her tights full of holes. She did not want to flash anyone in her attempt to get down.

Two men walked past her, arms around each other's shoulders and hair in each other's faces. They laughed as they walked past and disappeared into another door she hadn't noticed.

The slope flattened out and the tunnel turned to the right. Melanie breathed a sigh of relief and stood up. The lights were dim so she kept one hand on the wall as she walked forward. Around another corner she saw the door, taller than the one she had entered by, made of dark wood and lined with heavy metal rivets. Light slipped around the edges. Melanie paused and a cold breeze came up behind her, pushing her forwards. The smell of mildew faded the closer she got to the door, being replaced by the welcoming smell of an open wood fire. The door opened and light spilled into the corridor.

Melanie took a deep breath, inhaling the soft smell of wood smoke and the sour sharp smell of old beer. The bar was large and crowded tables filled the space. She edged forwards, her tights snagging on the splinters in the floor. She glanced down. The wood of the floor was marred with furrows as if a pack of sharp clawed wolves had dwelt here. Feeling eyes on her, Melanie glanced at the bar. A woman with sharp black eyes glared fiercely at her, causing her to flinch. The woman was bone thin, her greying hair pulled harshly back making her skeletal appearance much more prominent. Melanie almost fled under the glare but a hand on her back pushed her forwards.

'Pretty girl.' The boy smiled at her and steered her into the bar. 'Raywin, you frighten our first new face this Festival. How are we to live if you behave so?'

'Fool Munak, Nit has already served her.' The woman, Raywin, said 'served' in such a way that Melanie shivered. Munak clicked his tongue.

'Nit.' He looked to Melanie, smirked and jumped over the bar. 'Her drinks are sticky sweet.' He leaned closer till he was almost nose to nose with Melanie. 'I can give you something much nicer.' Melanie swallowed the lump in her throat and felt the heat in her belly claw its way up her neck and over her face. Munak's eyes wandered down her body and slowly back to her face. His smile widened.

'What do you recommend?' Melanie asked, triumphant that her voice remained steady. Munak's self satisfied smile became a smirk.

'Many things.' He turned and opened a cupboard filled with bottles. Melanie could still feel the burn of Raywin's glare and risked glancing at her out of the corner of her eye. Raywin was watching her but her look was no longer a glare, it was desperate. Melanie felt her throat clench, she couldn't breathe. The thump of a shot glass landing in front of her made her snap her eyes away from Raywin. Munak took her hand and wrapped it around the glass.

'You'll love this,' he promised. Melanie lifted the glass as goosebumps rose over her back and she shivered. The goosebumps remained as she glanced over her shoulder and caught the shadowed patrons watching her.

'Don't,' a voice whispered.

'Never mind them,' Munak drew her back to him. 'Old men watch pretty girls.' Melanie felt her face grow hot again and downed the shot to hide her blush from Munak. The drink tasted of salt and herbs and felt cool going down, but quickly turned to ice in her belly. Melanie flinched then the ice melted and as it did she felt herself melt with it. She glanced behind her again; no one was watching her now. She let out a little sigh and smiled at Munak.

'What was that?' She felt herself smirk.

'Tears of Seraph,' Munak grinned. 'Would you like another?'

'Munak,' Raywin snapped. 'She's not going anywhere now, go and clean the tables and put a plate down for Balor, you know how he likes to play at civilisation.' Munak sighed and glanced at Melanie.

'In a moment perhaps,' he said and lifted a rag he walked away.

'You really should not have done that,' a deep, sad voice said. Melanie flinched and saw no one near her. A small black cat hopped up onto the seat next to her and blinked big yellow eyes at her.

'Hello kitty,' Melanie said softly, reaching out to let the cat smell her fingers. It glanced at her hand, then back to her face, meeting her eyes fully.

'Hello,' it answered. Melanie let out a yelp and almost fell from her chair.

'...cat,' she managed, the ice in her veins helping to calm her shock that a small cat was talking to her. The black cat glanced at her shaking hands and chuckled.

'I am the least of your worries child,' the cat purred. Melanie frowned. 'You need to realize where you are.'

'Where I am?' Melanie reached out her hand and ran her shaking fingers over the cat's soft ink-coloured fur. Her fingertips tingled. 'Ok talking kitty, where am I?'

'In trouble,' the cat said.

"When cats start talking I think trouble is probably right. Laura will kill me if I'm this drunk already,' Melanie muttered. The cat laughed.

'Laura killing you is even less of a worry than I am, and I am trying to help you.' The cat arched as Melanie scratched its back.

'Take a look around. A proper look,' the cat purred. Melanie did so. She looked at the patrons huddled together around small tables. They were all old and thin, they looked frail but normal.

'Misfits,' the cat snorted. 'Ghouls and rejects, old and decrepit. They band together for safety and to hunt. They are like spiders, not fit to chase their prey, they trap them.'

Melanie looked again. The men and woman hunched over the tables were beyond thin, they were emaciated; the shadows around their eyes were not make up but bruising. She focused on an old man who like the others was thin, but he was holding a pipe. He trembled when Munak put an empty plate down in front of him. The cat followed her eye line and laughed bitterly.

'Old dragons should be killed rather than allowed to live on, no longer able to fly.' Melanie kept watching the old man. His pipe was not lit, yet smoke came from his mouth and nostrils when he breathed out.

'Tamrus you are frightening my customers,' Raywin said, coming over with another full glass in her hand. She set the glass in front of Melanie. Melanie went to lift it but Tamrus hissed and clawed at her hand. She dropped the glass, the drink spilled over the bar. One of the old men behind them cursed and spat at Tamrus who avoided it easily.

'I do not aim to frighten them you old Ghoul, I aim to warn.'

'Then maybe you should do it away from Balor's domain,' an old voice shouted from behind.

'That old goat knows I am here,' Tamrus smirked.

'I do not approve,' Raywin snarled. Tamrus shrugged and turned to Melanie.

'You do not see the place you have come to, you need to leave.' Tamrus looked down and Melanie followed his eyes to the marks on the floor. Melanie frowned and hopped down from the stool. She ran her fingers over the grooves in the wood floor. Her nails fit perfectly into the dips.

'Nails?' she said softly and followed the marks with her eyes. They ran to the door. 'Something was dragged.'

'No, claws. They have never needed to drag anyone. They are spiders who trap their prey, poison their prey.' Melanie looked at the spilt drink on the bar.

'I... I need to go.' Melanie stood and stumbled in her haste. She scrambled to the door; no one paid any head to her panic. She ran into the door and pulled hard on the cold metal handle. It didn't budge. Hands settled on her shoulders. Melanie looked up to see Munak.

'You've downed our drink and eaten our food. The door will not open for you.' Behind them Melanie heard a lot of chairs sliding back as the aged men got to their feet as one. Munak tightened his grip on her shoulders and turned her to face them.

'She did not eat.' Tamrus leapt down from the stool. 'She can open the door.'

'Yes she did.' Munak leaned forward; Melanie could see his cheek out of the corner of her eye. She could see his hands on her now, his fingers were impossibly long, tipped with terrifying claws. The aged men shuffled towards them with mouths agape and teeth bared, their limbs too long to be human.

'Balor,' Munak called. The giant man appeared as if from nowhere. He was suddenly in front of them, Raywin on his arm. Melanie heard herself whimper.

'She is the first of the Festival,' Raywin breathed. 'She is yours to devour my Lord.' Balor's mouth split into a savage grin.

AUTHOR'S NOTES

This collection of short stories began life as a group of authors from a writing forum deciding to publish their work together. In the early days of ebooks, when online indie publishing was still emerging into the world, I pulled the stories together as the editor and it turned into the anthology you see today.

I made a few suggested changes to each story, but also wanted to keep the unique voice and writing style of each author. Could each story be more polished? Yes, certainly (can't all our stories!). But I also wanted it to be a reflection of the stage each author had reached with their craft, captured in time and telling their story, their way.

The process of creating and publishing our work has helped us all grow as authors, and we are all proud of what we have achieved together.

We hope you enjoyed this insight into the start of our journey too.

AVAILABLE FROM AMAZON

Mullins Collection of Best New Fiction

A collection of nine short stories from nine different authors (plus two bonus tales from the editor). Experience the mystery and excitement of exploring a world populated with creatures unlike any you have ever seen - ghouls that feed in the darkness of the London underground in *The Orphaned City* and the strange patient who stalks the halls of a mental asylum in *Inferiority Complex*. Then discover why humans are the most curious species of all – the charming smile of the mysterious Jack in *Knowing Jack* and the devious mind of Red in *The Path I Set Upon*.

Travel between worlds bound together by an all-encompassing weave of storytelling. Fiction has the ability to create new worlds that reflect our lives in the real world. Each story in this collection offers a different perspective on human experience, a glimpse of who we really are, who we might have been, or who we wish to become. Will the next story scare you, or make you think differently about the world? Or will it spark into life a new idea, the kind that Jake develops from an overheard conversation in *Dreamworld*. Or question our very existence, like the revelations of Professor Westerham in *Reflection*. It might even lead to a dangerous hunt for untold riches, which Ryan experiences in *The Hassam Legacy*.

Whatever your tastes, this book holds a story for everyone. You may even discover a love for stories you wouldn't have considered before. Fiction does that to you. It draws you into its welcoming embrace. Sometimes the welcome is warm, like the strength of Helen after dealing with death in *Coming of Age*. Other times you feel an icy chill as the story grips you, like the terror that claws at Meg when she hears her parrot speak in *Scared to Death*. Either way, you'll always remember how you felt when you took your first step.

Nine different worlds are waiting to be explored. Each story hides a secret – a twist that awaits discovery by an adventurous reader.

Welcome to our worlds.

AVAILABLE FROM AMAZON

Mysteries and Misadventures: Tales from the Highlands

Ten tales set in the Highlands of Scotland.
True childhood secrets revealed in the Story Behind the Stories.

In *The Road Trip*, a couple make a surprise stop at a guesthouse with a deadly history, looking for its next victims. In *Secrets of the River*, an unopened box is dragged from the river. A hastily scrawled message from the past, stolen by a young woman who is now being hunted. With time running out, can she survive its secrets?

In *Equal To and Greater Than*, James has a 1 in 54 condition. Attacked and humiliated, he must harness the power of his gifts and become the hero he needs to be. In *The Gala Queen*, it's Halloween night. A prank goes wrong. A young girl dies and the boy responsible has got away with it. Until the annual town gala, when the gala queen comes seeking vengeance.

In *Revenge of the Green Man*, Charlie plots to get his stolen CD back, dragging his friend into ever-crazier schemes. In *The House on Lovers' Lane*, a boy is missing and two girls lie to their parents so they can spend the night drinking in a field. But when a dare goes wrong they soon discover the danger they are in.

In *Call of the Nuckelavee*, a woman stalks the sandy dunes, following the voice of her drowned father. In the turbulent sea, she comes face to face with a creature that has haunted her nightmares. In *Black Dog in the Devil's Bothy*, a troubled woman hikes through a storm. She strays from the mountain path and loses her way in the forest. Taking shelter in a bothy, she discovers her fears have followed her to the darkest of places.

In *Last Train South*, a woman boards a train with a heavy suitcase. Evidence she must dispose of, with the help of her friends. In *Stolen Peace*, a nuclear biologist just wants to spend his final days camping in the woods and reading his book. Unfortunately, trained killers want him to return the item he stole.

AVAILABLE FROM AMAZON

Scottish Urban Legends:
50 Myths and True Stories

A HUGE collection of Scottish Urban Legends, Myths and True Stories. The definitive guide to the legendary stories that reveal Scotland's mysterious past.

Each tale is dazzlingly retold for a modern audience. Gather around the fireside and hear stories from a land filled with magic and mystery. Feel the rich history brought to life through folktales passed down through generations. Hear the true stories that lurk amongst these myths, things that the author has witnessed with his own eyes, revealed for the very first time.

Where is the most haunted road in Scotland? Who got caught cheating while playing cards with the devil? Which military camouflage suit got its name from a forest faerie? What ancient rhyme can summon a violent poltergeist?

Roadside phantoms, cunning spirits and real-world killers, this enchanting collection has them all. From tales of great battles, to pagan rituals that are still performed today. Discover the locations where you can see and feel these experiences for yourself, if you dare.

Huddle closer to the fire, read the book and decide for yourself which of the legends are true.

AVAILABLE FROM AMAZON

Scottish Legends: 55 Mythical Monsters

A MAMMOTH collection of Scottish Legendary Creatures and Mythical Monsters. From Amazon bestselling author Aaron Mullins comes the ultimate guide to 55 fantastical creatures of Scottish folklore.

Discover the origins of each supernatural creature, from a land filled with werewolves, sea monsters and fiendish ghouls. Hear true accounts from people who have come face to face with these fearsome beasts and lived to tell their tale.

Stories of legendary creatures have always captured the imagination. The mythical unicorn is the national animal of Scotland and many travellers have gathered around campfires across Scottish hillsides to hear fascinating stories of mysterious blue men, sorcerous shapeshifters and ferocious sea serpents.

How can you tell if your child has become a changeling? Which female vampire hides her hooves from human eyes? Where can you capture a mermaid who will grant you three wishes?

Discover the answers to these questions and many more within this book.

AVAILABLE FROM AMAZON

Scottish Killers: 25 True Crime Stories

25 True Crime Stories of Murder and Malice

A fascinating collection of Scotland's most deadly serial killers and notorious murderers.

A chilling anthology of the true crime stories that shocked the world.

The details of each case are revealed.
The motives of each killer are explored.

Each murder is examined in a new light, stripped of the sensationalism of newspapers, and with the greatest amount of compassion and respect paid to the victims and their families.

This book analyses the minds of those who would commit such horrific crimes.

What drove Ian Brady to kill?
Which serial killer got away with 14 further suspected murders?
Which gangland killer became a successful Scottish artist?

Discover the answers to these questions in this book, where more difficult and devastating truths are also revealed.

THANK YOU

Thank you for reading my book! I always devote a lot of time to making my books as enjoyable as possible for you.

I have a day job working for a lovely charity, so I write on my days off and in the evenings once my daughter has gone to bed and my family duties are done for the day.

So if you enjoyed reading my book, please kindly take a minute to leave a nice review so others can discover me and my writing.

I really appreciate you supporting me as an author and it inspires me to write more books for you!

Amazon: amazon.com/author/aaronmullins

FOLLOW ME

Twitter: twitter.com/DrAaronMullins

Facebook: facebook.com/aaronmullinsauthor

Instagram: instagram.com/draaronmullins

Youtube: youtube.com/c/AaronMullins

Pinterest: pinterest.com/aaronmullinsauthor

HEAR IT FIRST

Head to my website and click the 'Follow' button to be notified when I publish a new blog post, or a new book!

www.aaronmullins.com

ABOUT THE AUTHORS

AARON MULLINS

Dr Aaron Mullins is an award-winning, internationally published psychologist. He's also an Amazon bestselling author known for exploring powerful psychological experiences in his books.

Aaron has a wealth of experience in the publishing industry, with expertise in supporting fellow authors achieve their writing goals. He started Birdtree Books Publishing where he worked as Editor-in-Chief. He also partnered with World Reader Charity, getting ebooks into Africa and sponsoring English lessons in an under-tree school in India.

Aaron taught Academic Writing at Coventry University and has achieved great success with his bestselling short story anthologies. He also writes non-fiction business and authorship guides for entrepreneurs and fellow writers.

Aaron's book *How to Write Fiction: A Creative Writing Guide for Authors* has become a staple reference book for writers and those interested in a publishing career.

Aaron's website, www.AaronMullins.com contains free resources to support authors with inspiration and practical help, with writing, publishing and marketing guides.

Aaron lives by the beach on the west coast of Scotland, where he devotes most of his non-writing time to charity work, travelling and exploring beautiful places that inspire him to write.

www.aaronmullins.com

ANGELA KELMAN

Angela Kelman lives with her family in Aberdeen, Scotland. She started writing seriously after being propelled into, what some people call, 'free time and coffee' - after her youngest of two boys began nursery. Angela writes short stories and in 2011 won August's competition on Writers billboard. She is now actively seeking publication for her first Young Adult/Fantasy Novel, The Kylo. As well as novels and short stories, Angela enjoys writing poetry - you can see examples of her work along with the blurbs for her novels on her website, available in the author contact section.

GARY STEWARD

Gary Steward was born in Yorkshire but has lived in Northumberland for over thirty years where he owns an art gallery. His writing began as lyrics for songs performed by his acoustic band in the north of England and as far as afield as Holland. Gary also sings in two choirs in his town. This is his first short story. He is married with two sons and two dogs.

KATE ROBINSON

Kate attended Aberystwyth University for 4 years, where she gained a law degree and post graduate diploma in legal practice. She spends her week days working as a paralegal and the rest of her time writing. She writes fantasy stories for young adults and hopes to provide stories that are a little different from the usual supernatural teen romance. She has a small orange cat called Mikho who is absolutely no help whatsoever.

Printed in Great Britain
by Amazon